NO LONGER
PROPERTY OF PPLD

JEASY
RUSS
PIKES PEAK LIBRARY DISTRICT
COLORADO SPRINGS CO 80901 – 1579
The trouble with baby.

156630253

The Trouble with Baby

BY MARISABINA RUSSO

Greenwillow Books
An Imprint of HarperCollins*Publishers*

The Trouble with Baby
Copyright © 2003 by Marisabina Russo Stark
All rights reserved. Manufactured in China.
www.harperchildrens.com

Gouache paints were used to prepare the full-color art.
The text type is Futura Book.

Library of Congress Cataloging-in-Publication Data

Russo, Marisabina.
The trouble with Baby / Marisabina Russo.
p. cm.
"Greenwillow Books."
Summary: Sam and his big sister Hannah have fun playing together, until Hannah gets a new doll for her birthday and begins paying so much attention to the doll that Sam gets jealous.
ISBN 0-06-008924-5 (trade). ISBN 0-06-008925-3 (lib. bdg.)
[1. Brothers and sisters—Fiction. 2. Dolls—Fiction.
3. Jealousy—Fiction.] I. Title.
PZ7.R9192 Tr 2003 [E]—dc21 2002067857

10 9 8 7 6 5 4 3 2 1 First Edition

PROPERTY OF
PIKES PEAK LIBRARY DISTRICT
P.O. BOX 1579
COLORADO SPRINGS, CO 80901

For Whitney

Hannah and Sam knew how to have fun together.
They had truck races.
They built cities out of blocks.
They painted pictures on brown paper that Mama
rolled out on the floor for them.

RE
Yellow
BLUE

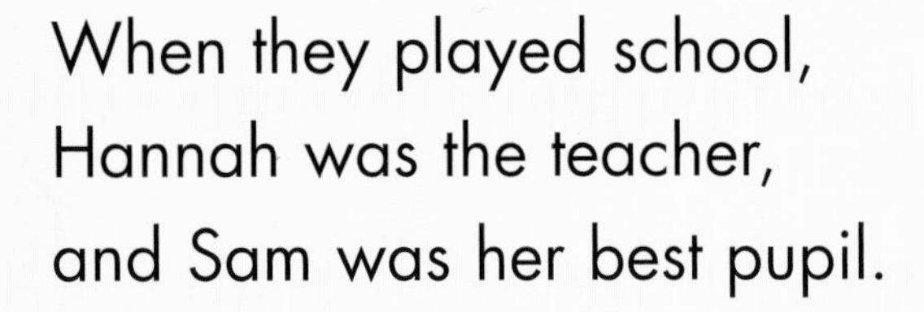

When they played school,
Hannah was the teacher,
and Sam was her best pupil.

When they made tents,
Sam called Hannah
through a long cardboard tube.

When it was almost time for bed,
they cuddled up with Daddy
so he could read a book to them.

On Hannah's birthday she had a party, and Sam was the only boy invited.
Sam watched Hannah open her presents: a box of magic tricks, a windup clown, a paint set, and a kite. Sam thought about how much fun they would have playing with Hannah's new toys. There was one more box left to open.

MAGIC

Hannah unwrapped the last gift and pulled out a doll. It was a baby doll, just the right size for Hannah to cradle in her arms. She kissed her new doll and squeezed her tight.

"I love this doll," said Hannah. "And I will name her Baby."

"Why don't you give your doll a real name, like Sarah or Jane?" asked Sam. "All your other dolls have real names."

"Baby is a real name," said Hannah.

"Can I look at her?" asked Sam.

"No," said Hannah. "Baby only wants me to hold her."

Instead of leaving Baby on the bed like all the other dolls, Hannah took her everywhere.

Baby sat on the kitchen table
while Hannah ate her cereal.

Baby sat on the sink
while Hannah brushed her teeth.

Baby rode in the car, sharing Hannah's seatbelt.
"Can't you go anywhere without Baby?" asked Sam.
"Baby doesn't like to be left alone," said Hannah.

Baby came with a pair of pajamas and a little plastic bottle.
Hannah decided to make some new clothes for Baby.
"Hannah, let's go outside and blow bubbles," said Sam.
"No," said Hannah. "I'm busy."

Hannah made a hat for Baby.
"That's not a hat," said Sam.
"That's an old mitten!"

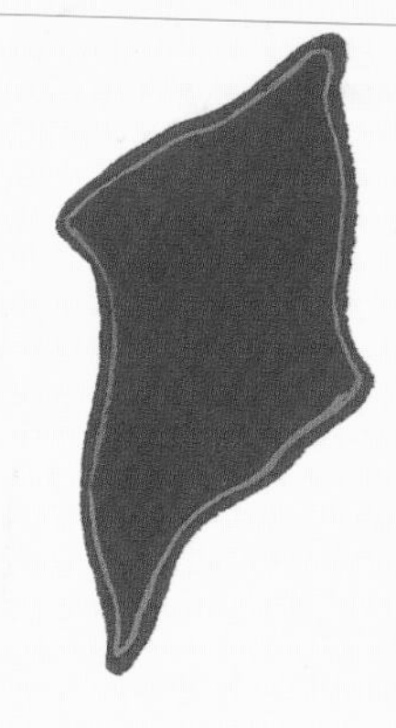

Hannah made a cape for Baby.
"That's not a cape," said Sam.
"That's an old washcloth!"

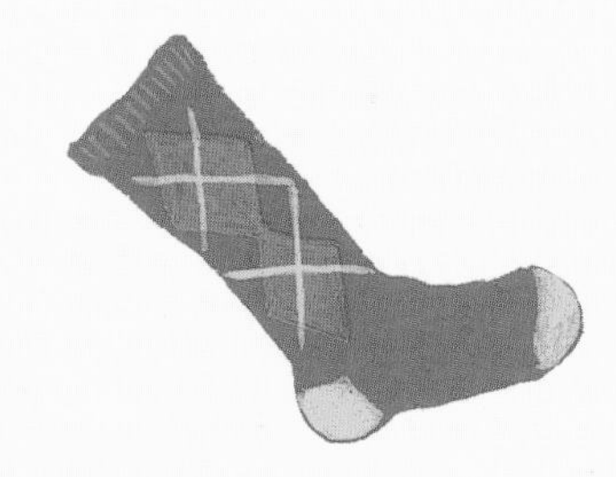

Hannah made a skirt for Baby.
"That's not a skirt," said Sam. "That's an old sock!"
"Shhh," said Hannah. "You'll hurt Baby's feelings."

After Baby had all her new clothes, Hannah said, "Now Baby can go to school."

Hannah set up two chairs, one for Sam and one for Baby. "Who can tell me a word that starts with the letter B?" asked Hannah.

Sam raised his hand. Baby just sat there. Hannah called on Baby.

"Butterfly?" said Hannah. "Yes, Baby, that is a very good answer."

"No fair!" said Sam. "Baby didn't say anything."

"Oh, yes, she did," said Hannah. "Baby is a very smart doll."

"I don't like it when Baby goes to school," said Sam. "Baby should sit on your bed with all the other dolls."

B
crayons

Hannah and Sam made tents in the living room. Sam called Hannah through the cardboard tube.

"Hello, Hannah," said Sam. "Would you like to come over for a visit to my tent?"

"Sure," answered Hannah. "Can I bring Baby?"

"No," said Sam. He was getting sick of Baby.

"Well, I don't have a baby-sitter, so I guess I can't come," said Hannah.

"She doesn't need a baby-sitter," said Sam. "Baby is only a doll."

One day Mama gave Hannah and Sam a big cardboard box.

"Let's make a jukebox," said Hannah.

They decorated the box with markers and cut holes for speakers. Hannah drew three buttons for three songs: one by her, one by Baby, and one by Sam.

"Baby can't sing," said Sam.

"Oh, yes, she can," said Hannah. "Baby is a very talented doll."

Jukebox
songs
1
Hannah
2
Baby
3

Daddy came along and
chose button number one.
Hannah sang a song
about a little red hen.

Mama chose button number two.
Baby sang a song about two cows
that go moo.
"Hey," said Sam. "That's not Baby
singing. That's you, Hannah!"

"Okay," said Mama. "Now it's time for song number three."

Sam began to sing.

"Baby, Baby, I hate you!
You look like a lobster
And you smell like one too!"

"Sam!" said Hannah. "You made Baby cry. She's never going to play with you again, and neither am I!"

"Good," said Sam.

The next day everything was different. Hannah played school only with Baby. Baby was a perfect student, but playing school with Baby was boring.

Hannah went into her tent, and she didn't call Sam. He didn't call her either. Playing tents without their cardboard tube phone was lonely.

Hannah played jukebox. She tried to teach Baby "Row, Row, Row Your Boat," but whenever Baby began to sing, Hannah had to stop singing her own part.

"Row, Row, Row Your Boat" just didn't sound right in only one voice. Playing jukebox without Sam was no fun at all.

Hannah went to Sam's room. She knocked on the door.

"Go away," said Sam.

"What are you doing?" asked Hannah.

"Playing a game," said Sam.

Hannah opened the door. Sam was on the floor with a game of Chinese checkers.

His big teddy bear was sitting nearby.

"Quiet," said Sam. "It's Teddy's turn."

Sam jumped a few marbles. "Good job, Teddy!"

"Can we play too?" asked Hannah. "Baby and me?"

Sam looked at Hannah and Baby.

Then he looked at Teddy.

"Teddy says it's okay with him," said Sam. "As long as he gets to go first."

"But Teddy is only a bear," said Hannah.

"A very smart bear," said Sam.

After Chinese checkers,
they played school.

After school,
they played in their tents.

After tents, they played jukebox.
Hannah drew a new button on the box for Teddy's song.
Hannah and Sam decided to add another song that they could sing together. Now there were five songs.
Sam arranged Teddy and Baby on the floor as the audience.
Then along came Mama and Daddy.

"Look, there are two new songs on the jukebox," said Mama.

"Play number five," said Sam.

Daddy pressed the button.

Hannah started singing "Row, Row, Row Your Boat" in her best voice. Sam came in at exactly the right place.

"That is one of my favorite songs," said Mama.

"You are two very talented children," said Daddy.

"Let's sing it again," said Hannah.

Jukebox
songs
1 Hannah
2 Baby
3 Sam
4 Teddy
5 Hannah + Sam

And so they did.